A COIN BY THE GRAVE

A COIN BY THE GRAVE

IVY SAMUEL

Matador
9 De Montfort Mews
Leicester LE1 7FW, UK
Tel: (+44) 116 255 9311 / 9312
Email: books@troubador.co.uk
Web: www.troubador.co.uk/matador

ISBN 978-1906221-850

Typeset in 12pt Times by Troubador Publishing Ltd, Leicester, UK

Matador is an imprint of Troubador Publishing Ltd

In loving memory of my beloved husband Shah Nawaz al Huque

Many thanks to the Joint Council for the Welfare of Immigrants for permission to refer to their handbook on Immigration, Nationality and Refugee Law.

CHAPTER ONE

The hearse arrived slowly and reluctantly at the doorway, and Carol expecting its arrival, emerged to meet it. The door of the hearse swung open, and out sprung two men, one of whom opened the rear door. A very few mourners had arrived almost simultaneously, one bearing a huge wreath with many red roses and other types of flowers, woven with care. There was someone holding her shoulders, urging her forward to look at the body inside the coffin from the rear door. In complete numbness she moved towards it, her steps like those of a robot. The coffin was only partially open to reveal the face and upper part of the body which was swaddled with white cloth. Devoid of feeling, she looked at the face of her husband in a detached manner as if he was someone she had known some time ago. It was as if her own spirit had come out of her body and was hanging around watching.

His face was pale, so serene, and almost angelic with the white cloth draped over his body. She could only stare at his face, stare and stare. The silence around was rudely interrupted by two teenage Kosovan boys who were kicking a tin can on the pavement opposite and laughing, seemingly indifferent to the picture of grief before them, not giving a damn. There was no respect for the dead.

There was not a flicker of compassion in the eyes of the two men standing near the hearse, who were looking at their watches, shuffling their feet with annoyance at the delay, impatient to be gone.

One of her friends squeezed her arm as the coffin was closed. The two men jumping in, the hearse started to move. Carol and her family piled into a waiting car driven by the priest. Panic seemed to register itself and she whispered to him, "follow the hearse closely and don't lose sight of it please, in case they take him away where I can't reach him." The friend sitting in front with the priest, nodded reassuringly. Carol focussed on the hearse in front, oblivious to everything else. She had to be close, so very close.

They reached Carpender's Park, and Carol walked towards the hearse already there. The two men looked at her, and when requested to be allowed just to stand near it, they shook their heads. This is England for God's sake, and this was her husband lying inside, yet two foreigners seemed to take charge of the situation, denying her a final chance to say goodbye. How dare they! Had not the body been taken from the hospital where he breathed his last the day before? She had then placed a brief kiss on the already cold lips, her fingers ruffling his hair cursorily which already seemed damp, and then gently soothing his shoulder. There was no chance for a proper goodbye, no chance for the body to be brought back to the house, no chance to cradle him in her arms and whisper words of love.

The coffin was taken out, lowered into the ground, some words of prayer uttered, and the earth piled on top. It was over. Carol shed no tears. She could hear her son overwhelmed with grief, crying his heart out loudly, and she reached for him and held him close to her.

She looked around for her youngest daughter aged eleven, and saw her being comforted by her best friend.

The hearse was soon driven away, and her two in laws left as well. Carol was left with her two children, the priest and some of her friends. The priest conducted prayers with great fervour. Carol then knelt at the grave, and just for awhile, a chink of reality cracked her shell of numbness. Her tears sprouted out, trying to defrost this numbness. She gave a wild loud scream which pierced the air, shattering the silence around. She could hear her scream echoing throughout the air. She screamed out his name over and over again, willing him to get up and hug her once more, just once more.

She felt warm hands trying to pull her away, and finally yielded after a long tussle. She was bundled into the car and as she plonked herself on to the seat, she suddenly stopped crying, as if a great slab of ice had covered this fountain of grief, to be slowly thawed over a period of ten years.

That night, Carol and her two children, together with her two in laws, slept on mattresses in the living room, unison in their grief. During the night Carol often got up to hug her knees, and with low agonising groans, rocked herself backwards and forwards, feeling that if she did not do so, she would die. Sheer physical exhaustion having got the better of her, she fell into a fitful sleep.

Then deep into the night, the sound of a ringing of a small bell seemed to come from the room she had shared with her late husband. Carol got up with a start, and her son who was asleep next to her, also woke up. He went towards the door and must have soon realized that his father was dead, for he stopped in his tracks, and lay down again. Indeed a small bell had been placed on the table next to the bed when he was ill, and he used to ring it at times when he was on his own, if he wanted anything or anyone. The sound was eerie but seemed to indicate that his spirit would always be around.

CHAPTER TWO

People react to grief in different ways, some bizarre, some unbelievable, wafted by a wave over which they seemingly have no control. For many days after her husband's death, Carol would wake up with a feeling of nausea, as if something was welling up within her, curdling her stomach and rising upwards, ready to suffocate and choke her. She wanted to retch but could not. A wave of temporary madness swept over her. She was grieving and could not help or comfort her children. Dear God! She wished she could. As far as possible she never mentioned her husband to her children, and when they mentioned him, she would change the subject. To well wishers who politely enquired after his health, she spoke of him as if he was alive. Sadly the youngest daughter followed suit.

Only those having lost a parent or partner in a foreign land, can understand the complete desolation of having no relatives or extended family around, whose presence might have filled a little void in their hearts. Carol's in laws once the funeral was over, soon distanced themselves from her family and from her, unhappy that their late brother being so besotted with Carol, had allowed her freedom of thought and beliefs. There was tremendous support from church members but they were not family.

"If only she would cry" whispered her friends, "it might help her." Carol hardly shed tears, refusing to believe that her beloved had passed on. Occasionally when she visited the shops and her eyes dwelt on something that he had loved to eat, would she battle with her grief and try hard not to break down. It ended in her eventually collapsing into a flood of tears, to the consternation of other shoppers. She had to be led away by her children.

She became disorientated, often losing her bearings whenever she went out. Worried about her, the children would wait anxiously for her return. They were so pleased when she eventually returned safe.

Why this terrible rage that soon shook her? She ranted against the Creator for his death, and also directed her rage against her two children without realizing that they were hurting too. Just before her husband had a cardiac arrest at home, he had called out to his son to have breakfast with him, but as was his nature, he took time to answer although he was in the kitchen close by. Carol awakened from her sleep to call him, only to notice that her husband was going into cardiac arrest. He was later rushed to hospital by paramedics, only to die a few weeks later. She accused her son of being a murderer.

The poor boy listened to her rantings and remained silent, obviously feeling that he was in some way to blame. What can one say to a woman temporarily out of her mind!

Then there came another feeling of wanting to escape because of an inability to cope. She travelled to her own country for a while on her own, returned, and then left again for a few weeks. Each time she returned, she would rush to the grave in anticipation and speak to him. He was still alive, he was just sleeping: he could hear her.

"Poor thing, she cannot accept that he has gone," said one of her friends.

At other times she would lie on the grave, asking him to come out and to hold and kiss her. When news of her behaviour and marked grief had reached her doctor, she suggested a referral to a psychologist in her clinic and Carol reluctantly agreed. She was put off by his approach when he said, "how can I help you." Was she a customer at the shop waiting to be served? In any case what remedy could he give for a broken heart? She vented her rage at him. However the long and short of this interlude was that he diagnosed her grief to be frozen and lay at the back of her neck. She never stepped foot at his office again.

One would have thought that a person caring for a loved one, always on the brink of death, would have been prepared for the worst. In nursing him after various heart operations, and knowing how ill he was, Carol had stared defiantly at death in the eye, although she had touched its shroud and smelt its chill. But when death eventually struck, it was a total disbelief, a shock, as if she had partaken of a potent poison causing a terrible heartache and numbness of all her senses.

The strange part of this was that in his own way he had been preparing her for his death. About a month before his cardiac arrest, Carol had mentioned to him, "can you believe this; my sister has married again just two months after her husband's death." He studied her closely and softly replied, "I don't think I will mind if you married again." Carol was a bit shaken and could not make a reply.

At another time he mentioned "don't take me to the church darling." She knew what he was referring to and felt an answer was due. " I will do whatever you wish."

"We will not be buried together will we?" She did not reply for she was unable to say anything or to think of death. He had known full well of their different religious upbringing. Was he hinting that he was going to die? No it can't be. She continued to remain silent. Yes, said Carol within herself, don't think of death and it will not happen.

As she cuddled up to him one evening, pushing her face close to his neck, he said, "I just don't know what you are going to do when I am gone."

Just the night before his cardiac arrest, he came

to the living room and asked her hesitatingly to come to bed, and while there, amongst other things he said, “we have been together through thick and thin.”

“I love you” she said, offering him some tea from her cup. “I lovc you too” he replied, and took a sip of the tea. On hindsight, that was his saying goodbye .

At the hospital next day, Carol was with him. There were so many tubes attached to him, and he had an oxygen mask over his mouth. Carol bent down and put her face close to him and said, “Hi.” He raised both palms over her cheeks, and she nuzzled her cheeks in that embrace. His hands fell weakly to his side, and over his mask he looked at her with eyes full of love. Their eyes held as if for eternity. This was his final goodbye, after which he slipped into temporary and then permanent coma.

CHAPTER THREE

How does one deal with a situation when a mother cannot reach out to her children when death strikes? Can a woman temporarily deranged, ever be able to draw her children close and put their interests before her grief? Carol ran the house as seemed normal outwardly and tried to play the role of mother and father, but with no success. Her eleven year old daughter must have sensed that there was no one to comfort her, and perhaps tried to get comfort from somewhere else. She became disobedient and started to come home late from school, got into bad company, and the situation turned into a nightmare. Friends from the church tried to help, but things began to spiral out of control.

One day an old car like a withered woman, managed to reach Carol's gate, grunting and belching. Out of it sprang Eddie and Jasmine, two of Carol's close friends. They kicked the car, harassed at her erratic behaviour, and glad to have finally made it to the house. They looked at each other nervously, pressed the door bell, and wondered how Carol was going to react to the disturbing news they were going to dish out to her. Would she crack under the strain of the impending news they wondered uneasily, or would she continue to act like an ice maiden smiling at grief. If only she would cry, damn her. It was already three months since her husband had passed away.

Giving them a smile that hardly reached her eyes, Carol ushered them into the living room. She sat down on the sofa quietly, outwardly calm. They had to avert their gaze from her face, for the eyes that gazed at them revealed intense suffering and agony of soul. "We have come to take you to the police station as your daughter has been detained for assaulting a girl."

"Whose daughter… which police station?" she queried almost mechanically, as if the matter concerned someone whom she really did not know.

"Floss is at the police station. It is not far away. We will take you there," Eddie said kindly.

Carol reached for her coat, as if it was something she had done in everyday life, and followed them into the car. She remained quiet throughout, and only when they were nearing the police station did she offer the question, "how is she?"

The policeman at the desk asked her to sign some papers which she did with trembling fingers. It triggered off a mild asthma attack. The rear door was ordered to be opened so as to enable her to breathe in some fresh air. Ravishing scents perhaps from a garden close by, drifted in as if determinedly, and engulfed over her. She was then led to a cubicle where her daughter was, looking frightened and upset.

Carol was invited to go into the interview room where an interview was to be recorded on tape. Floss looked at her pleadingly, as if begging for understanding. Carol let her gaze drift to the officer conducting the interview and noticed that he had dark hair streaked with grey. She wondered whether he ever washed it: yes, she decided, it needed to have a good wash.

The interview came to an end, and being a minor, her first offence and extenuating circumstances, Floss was given a written caution, and allowed to leave. Was her daughter's behaviour a cry for help? She realized that her daughter must be grieving, but how could she give comfort when she herself could not function properly and unable to receive comfort.

If only her mother-in law was alive. In their efforts to nurse her beloved husband, a strong bond was established between them, born out of mutual love for him. There was a language barrier but they understood each other. Her mother-in law was a devout Muslim and they had only met when her son was critically ill. She sensed that Carol seemed to be of a different faith but encouraged her to pray accordingly. How pure that women was, how serene on her knees. Carol mused that if she was alive, she would be their source of comfort.

When they reached home, after thanking her friends for their time and support, Carol never discussed the matter further with her daughter, but instead asked her to have a bath and something to eat.

CHAPTER FOUR

During her period of grief, Carol was caught up by circumstances that were totally beyond her control. A frightening loneliness descended upon her, that for some reason could not be filled by the company of her children. The sound of laughter among couples around her, brought back memories of other laughter, memories of ecstasies and physical joys she had shared with her late husband. She had remembered the threads of their laughter, spinning a rainbow around them. With loneliness came a sort of vulnerability.

Two men accidentally came into her life. The first was John, thin, tall and kind, a very good listener. Carol found herself able to speak to him of her grief, and for the first time, slightly later than a year, tears rushed out like niagra. His strong hands massaged the tension from her back. The other man Leon was full of humour. Somehow or the other one thing led to another and she ended up in the arms of both of them at different times. This was always accompanied by a flood of tears, guilt and remorse. How could she have succumbed to all this, she who had never looked at another man in all her married life?

Carol picked up the phone and rang Kathleen. "I feel rotten and I need to talk: I can't live with myself."

"Meet me at the café Nero at Kilburn four sharp, and we will talk." She put down the phone.

She was there big as life. Carol rushed in, the traffic making her late, and apologised profusely. “Hope you haven’t been waiting too long.”

“About half an hour and two minutes if you must know. Sit down and take a deep breath.” They talked of various things and Carol then blurted out what was troubling her.

“I met a man and we got talking and soon the topic strayed to my recent bereavement. He is so funny and I couldn’t help laughing at some of his jokes. He is divorced and has known unhappiness, though of a different kind. After a few meetings, I found myself sleeping with him. It is not that I enjoyed it, but I had a terrible need for a man’s comfort, to snuggle against a broad shoulder and to have the warmth of a man’s arms around me.”

“There’s no need for this guilt. It’s a need, a remembrance of what it was like in the past.”

“But that’s not all. Almost at the same time I met someone else, quiet and soft-spoken, and went with him on a short cruise. You know the rest. I ended crying for hours and could not explain why."

"People cope with grief in different ways. Anyway your husband is dead and it is the living you should think about. What about your children? They need you to be strong for them. All this morality is not good for you anyway. For God's sake try to cry more. This bottling of grief is going to kill you."

"Strange thing this sex business. Your heart is broken and yet your body responds to a man. I will never understand it."

"Listen, I know you love the countryside, so why don't you come down to my place for the weekend and bring the kids? My parents will be away and we will have the house all to ourselves."

"Thanks, Kathleen, I would like to. You have made me feel better already. I won't forget to bring the tit bits you like. Best be going."

"Chin up mate, see you."

CHAPTER FIVE

"Gee Kathleen, your place is wonderful! Oh! The lovely smell of the countryside."

"Here's a batch of scones you especially like. Tuck in and relax in the garden. I am going to play a game of monopoly with your children. They have warned me not to cheat!"

Carol sat on the wooden bench at the end of the garden. A sense of stillness prevailed all around. A row of conifer trees stood majestically all the way on the side of the garden facing the road, deliberately planted that way to prevent prying eyes from invading the privacy of the home. The transparent green house seemed to apologise for not offering anything on display, but a few potted plants with young leaves sprouting upwards.

The old apple tree in the middle of the garden, gloated triumphantly, with its burst of hundreds of pink flowers. It was April, and other plants in the garden were breaking into bud, seeming to challenge the world to stop their impending bloom. Neko the golden retriever, lay sprawled on the virgin grass.

Nearby could be heard the chorus of birds, the chaffinch, robin and blackbirds, each in different pitch, as they perched high on still bald trees close by. There was a hint of expectancy in the air and her thoughts began to drift to her childhood days. A cocktail of emotions flashed through her as she cast her mind back to those days.

There were eleven children in the family, and Carol was one of the youngest. Her father a disciplinarian, had fixed ideas of how his children should behave. It was unheard of in those days to disobey one's parents, and she sometimes wished that she could exchange him for someone else who never used the cane. She had a patient mother whom he adored. It was a love marriage. Her father used to tell her as a child, that there were problems in his family when he married her mother, for she was of Western origin. Intermarriage was not on the cards at that time.

It was difficult to understand why her father, a professional man and who had his later education in London, would object to a television or radio being used in the house, deeming that the time should be better used by the children in preparing for exams.

How little did he know what they did when she and her three other siblings arrived home from school in the afternoons. After having their lunch, they comfortably waited to hear the snores of their mother who always enjoyed her afternoon siesta. They then enjoyed a field day, heralding the neighbouring children that it was safe to come out and play rounders. These children after popping their heads out of the window, succumbed to their call to play. They improvised on the rules of the game to make it more exciting. If the ball fell and was picked up by the fielder, it could be thrown directly at the person running, after having batted. This was the best part of the game, for sometimes the ball would be picked up from the narrow open drains surrounding the house. Imagine the stain on their clothes. Mercifully the ball missed its destination many times. No one minded that their clothes were stained with mud or whether they stank. The thrill of the game was to make a full run without getting hurt.

Excitement would spill over as the game went into full swing, often awakening her mother who recognizing her hysterical screams, would shout from her room for her to come in from the sun. The children held their tongues hoping she would go back to sleep, which she usually did. They then continued.

Unfortunately, sometimes their play would come to a halt at the sight of a car which slowly began to negotiate its way into the driveway. Out stepped the violin teacher who was a tall thin man with a squeaky voice. His presence would throw her into a panic as she hardly practised her violin. She never remembered when he was due and was unfortunate to be always the first one among her siblings to be picked out to begin the lesson. It was as if he had a suspicion that she might otherwise disappear. There was no time to change her clothes or look presentable. He used to look at her, shaking his head, her hair wet with sweat, her feet bare, and dress marked with traces of a wet dirty ball!

There were countless times when he would tweak her ear if she struck a wrong note. Her other three siblings were rewarded with praise and smiles for their good efforts. They had sufficient time to appear presentable by the time their turn came. In truth, when they played their violin, even the dog used to howl at the sound of such lovely music. She was lucky that her father returned home from work after five, and the lessons began about three.

She smiled at the recollection of countless times when she got herself into mischief. There were squabbles and lots of playful teasing with her other three siblings. Her older sister Danielle had one day fallen asleep on the huge dining table, with one ear exposed for the world to see. Finding a tiny beaker close by with a little milk in it, she slowly approached the tempting ear and poured a drop or two into it, causing her to bounce up like a rocket and frantically to dig into her ear. Needless to say she had flashed past her, lucky to be alive.

One another occasion her sister Octavia had called her a skinny rabbit, and as retribution, she spat into her food. It was not that she was badly behaved, but she had a fiery temper and was very impulsive. In a fit of rage Octavia screamed, “ look at what Carol has done; she spat into my food and I’m not eating this.”

Georgina her other sibling, never stopped complaining at tea time, and used to drive the maids up the wall. Carol had recollected with a smile how on one such occasion, not knowing what possessed her, she had dipped her small finger into her sister’s cup of tea, pretending it was an accident. It was no accident and Georgina who knew this, was outraged. By the time her mother turned around to redress the situation, she had slipped under the huge table, crawled out from the other side and had disappeared.

Carol clearly remembered that her father was a snob, and she had to refuse many invitations to parties by her school friends from lower social backgrounds. She clearly resented this. Summoning his four youngest children one day he said, “never let me catch you mixing with that Indian family down the end of the road." He was referring to a poor family consisting of three young girls with a middle aged mother who never smiled, but who tended to her cows all day. Her other three siblings were not interested in going there anyway, for they did not like to play hop scotch, which involved kicking a stone on to squares drawn by chalk, on the ground.

Carol smiled at the recollection of how much she was addicted to this game as a child, and could not resist going there to play at the expense of incurring her father's wrath. The best way to shift the stone from one square to another was to play with bare feet. Once she was engaged in the game, nothing else mattered except the stone and the squares. In the excitement of the game, she never felt any pain, although her toes were bleeding. Her toes hurt so much later when she put on her shoes to make her way towards home, that she found it difficult to walk. One or other of her sisters would cover for her, and would religiously call her to come away before their father was due back from work. About ten yards away, there would be a prolonged scream like a god in pain. “Caroool, Caroool!” Surely that voice could be heard from a mile!

She was always sorry to have her game cut short, and in her haste to return home, would sometimes tread over the piles of dung left by the cows. Sometimes she lost her balance and her feet plunged into the freshly laid dung. She had no alternative but to throw away the offending shoes. Sometimes she chose to ignore her sister’s warnings who then, would draw slowly nearer to her and say, “if father sees what you are doing, he will take your skin off, and we will all get into trouble.”

Unfortunately, one day, her father returned home earlier than usual and all hell broke loose. Standing there at the gate to greet her as she ran home was her father. In his hand he held four canes of different width and gave her the choice of one of them. She chose the thinnest, thinking it would hurt her less. It hurt the most and four lashes were imprinted on her outstretched palm. There was the added humiliation of the incident being witnessed by others as they passed by.

The old Chinese grandmother living next door who on seeing this, and shocked at this display of violence, hastily approached him, and gesticulating with her arms screeched in Chinese, "kick your mother's arse! You wicked devil," she continued.

Carol smiled at the occasion when she called her father "botha," the Malay word for "baldhead". Indeed, he was practically bald with only a fringe of hair on both sides of his head. Whether it was an insult to his vanity, or the shock that any of his children would dare to speak to him like that, he ordered the maid to bring him a cane which was delivered promptly. The incident happened near the big dining room table, which was very long and had two rounded ends. It had to be huge as the family was large.

It was then a game of cat and mouse. He began by chasing her and, as if her life depended on it, she fled round the table, her youth and agility in her favour. She was tiny and managed to shoot beyond the reach of the cane. Not being able to catch her, he enlisted the help of two maids. They were a special breed of Chinese maids who wore long white tunics with black trousers, and who had their long hair tied in a single plait. Their job was to oversee the work done by other maids in the house, and to make sure that visitors were well received.

They were necessarily of calm disposition. Having been summoned to intercept her, they half-heartedly placed themselves at certain positions along the table, their arms outstretched. As she sprinted round the table she was able to ward them off by pushing them aside or by knocking against their flat chests, their breasts like fried eggs. Many a time under the impact, they would almost topple over as they were petite. They loved her very much and hated to see her suffer.

It was a matter of time before she was caught, but in her fear did not feel the sting of two strokes of the cane lashed at her by her father, who by this time, was breathing heavily with exhaustion and damaged pride. The two maids then ushered her into their room, administered a balm for the stripes, shaking their heads sadly as they did so.

CHAPTER SIX

Carol was offered a life line when she converted from being a Barrister to that of a solicitor, and allowed to set up her own firm. She was interested only in dealing with asylum cases, as she felt strongly for those fleeing from persecution in their own land. She began with a few cases under the Legal Aid Scheme and soon her popularity grew. She was so busy, worked long hours, and was glad she did not have time to think of her late husband. She did not want to think about him and this work load prevented her from going crazy. There was so much work involving an asylum case, and she found herself sinking into her bed late at night, very exhausted. She was often awakened early some mornings, by telephone calls from the interpreters that they were bringing a few clients when the office opened.

Through dealing with the asylum seekers, her healing process began to take place slowly. Many of the asylum seekers suffered horrific physical injuries and emotional trauma. As she listened to their tales, it made her realize that she had much to be thankful for, as she had a happy marriage. The children of the refugees have commented at occasional times, that their pets had been disembowelled in Kosovo and their entrails shown to them. These experiences have haunted them. Carol used to keep some money of her own in the drawer of her desk, which she gave to the parents for their children, so that they could buy some food and necessities.

In most asylum cases it is the interpreters that bring the work for which they are paid under the Legal Aid Scheme. To her consternation Carol was later informed that some interpreters knowing the clients to be vulnerable, would try to squeeze extra money from them despite having been paid by Legal Aid. This was especially so in the case of a few Chinese clients who depended very heavily on the interpreters. Many in their desire to escape from China, had made use of agents who provided all the necessary documents for them to enter the United Kingdom. Their relatives in China had to pay the initial deposit for them, and the rest to be paid by the asylum seekers when they found a job at the United Kingdom. There was no escaping the balance owed, and those who defaulted would often be kidnapped and ill treated.

At one point Carol took one of the interpreters to task after being informed that he had taken extra money from the client. She refused to take any more Chinese clients from him and never let him step into the office again.

"Wrong move," said a friend also legally trained. "You are providing a rod for your own back. What happens outside the office is not your business. You don't know half of what happens outside a solicitor's office."

"I can't help it, these people have suffered enough and should not be further exploited."

Make no mistake that if Carol found any discrepancy in their statements, she would question the clients about this and demand an explanation. One Pakistani client answered in English which she could just about understand, that the interpreter had written out his statement for him and that was all he knew. Obviously the interpreter denied this.

Ahmed the legal representative returned from the interview at the Home Office one evening, and placed a copy of the interview notes on Carol's desk. He appeared disgusted and angry, complaining that the interviewing officer was unreasonable in his questioning of the client, and that some of the questions were blatantly unfair.

“How can he insist that the client should have made his claim known to the immigration officer on arrival? Obviously he is not enlightened enough to realize that many asylum seekers do not know the correct procedure to do so, and are afraid of being turned away. He was deliberately trying to discredit his account.”

Carol had herself attended various interviews, and found several interviewers to be aggressive or dismissive, and used to protest at this at the end of the interview. Many of them were actually ignorant of the basic conditions of the country from which the asylum seekers have fled, causing her to fret, as she knew that the contents of the asylum interviews contributed largely to the decisions made by the Home office.

“Did you listen to the public debate about asylum over the television yesterday?” asked one of her fellow solicitors.

“I have given up bothering to do so. They flavour of prejudice and their comments are misleading. You will notice that asylum issues are often raised at election times to divert the people's attention from the real issues. It is just a gimmick. Of course you will also find the media playing on the emotions of the public, and politicians like Enoch Powell selling himself in his comments of "rivers of blood". What people need to know is that if asylum seekers are ever given permission to work, they are usually paid less than the local people, and are given jobs that these people do not want to do."

"Yes, the government is one of the signatory states to the Refugee Convention, and she is obliged to follow it. People should not think that asylum seekers can just walk into the UK and get asylum. They have to comply with the Convention. They must be outside their country, have a well founded fear of persecution due to religion, race, nationality, membership of a social or political group or are unable or unwilling to obtain the protection of the country."

Carol also added that the Human Rights Act made applicable to Britain was subjcct to restrictions, to strike a balance between individual freedom and collective interests, and the courts often allowed restrictions to apply. Measures have often been adopted to prevent and deter asylum seekers from coming to Britain by detention, fast tracking, visa regimes and carrier's liability, to name a few, and restrictive access to government support. The public seem to wrongly believe that asylum seekers have all benefits and accommodation to the detriment of the local people.

While discussing with Alan another immigration lawyer, about the refusal of the Legal Services Commission to fund the attendance of representatives or clerks at asylum interviews from April 2004, he said, "this is detrimental to the asylum seeker, for many of them do not speak English. Have you noticed the poor standard of English of some of the interpreters employed by the Home Office? My interpreters had to intervene on a few occasions as their interpretation was not correct."

The phone rang and Carol stopped talking to take the call, glad to find it was not from a client but from a dear friend inviting her to her flat at Chelsea. The friend concluded by saying, "don't forget, Saturday, anytime in the morning. Put it in your diary."

CHAPTER SEVEN

Carol arrived at Amber's tiny apartment on Saturday in August as planned. As soon as she rang the bell, the door opened and Amber sprang into Carol's arms. There was no formality between them for they had been friends for years. Amber did not have spectacular features, but her face had a glow which radiated goodwill and beauty of the soul. Carol was swept into the small living room decorated with small paintings and ornaments. It was a warm day and the sun shone through the open windows, a ray of light focussing on the statue of Buddha, enhancing his benevolent smile. The atmosphere oozed with tranquillity. There was a sofa and two chairs unbelievably still in good condition, considering the numerous times her circle of friends plonked themselves on them.The three colourful rugs adorning the floor had seen better days. Her friends never noticed this, only too pleased to sprawl themselves on top of these when there were too many visitors around. They were just glad of her company.

It was that sort of place where her friends often popped in for a chat on the off chance that she would be at home, many of them not giving a moment's notice of their arrival. Amber worked as a receptionist at an embassy, and it was her sensible attitude to life that first attracted Carol to her. After talking about various trivial matters, noticing Carol's forlorn face she said, "you must come to terms with your husband's death and move on. It is way too long to continue to grieve like this. He is gone and that's that."

"If only I had a chance to say a proper goodbye. Instead, as soon as he passed away, he was out of my reach and his body buried within twenty four hours."

"Yes I know. It must have been awful for you, but that is the Muslim way of doing things and you have honoured his request concerning his burial."

"If I was born a Muslim and grew up in its teachings I would be able to understand in a more meaningful way its concept of death and burial, and accepted it. My husband was not a practising Muslim and I didn't know much about his religion, only that it taught you what was right and what was wrong."

A ring at the door made them both start and Amber said, "who on earth is that?" as she went to open the door. In barged Nina and Tim, who were also friends of Carol. Tim lifted Amber and swung her around like a rag doll. He watched Carol's face, and asked, "what's up?"

"Oh, nothing much, Carol and I were

discussing something about the Muslim religion."

"Shoot the fanatics, eh Carol? Pull off all their veils and head scarves."

All of a sudden some sort of loyalty crept unbeckoned into Carol's heart. True she only converted to a Muslim to be able to marry in a Muslim state, true her husband was a non practising Muslim, but that was his religion. She found herself replying, "if I am not mistaken Tim, there are fanatics in every religion. No religion teaches you to do wrong, and all worship the Great Being whatever name they chose to call it. Fanaticism of any sort, although it may not be expressed in acts of terror, can be just as damaging. Christian leaders in some denominations appear to twist the words of the Bible, by giving their own interpretation of it, and some try to introduce concepts which they think are right but does not seem to tally with the Bible. Sections of the congregation are brainwashed and fear to do anything not approved by the church."

Nina who so far had been listening to the conversation, chipped in and said, "all this tension between Muslims and Christians here, seems to boil down to the fact that each feels threatened by the other. Politicians hoping to win votes and adverse media publicity, have whipped up public feelings to ridiculous heights against the Muslims, tarring them all with the same brush. The world will be a better place if all religions are tolerated and respected. While it may be reported widely that the Muslim crusade is targeted against Western nations who embrace the Christian faith, many Christian churches target the Muslim faith in their own quiet way by saying it is tainted and a threat. Bear in mind that not so long ago the missionaries went to various nations with a Bible in one hand and a sword in another. I don't go a bundle over religious leaders of any faith, their motto being, 'do as I say but don't do as I do'."

Carol nodded her head and added, "you can say that again. When I was very young, my parents allowed Christian missionaries to live at our house for free, as they said they preached by faith and had no salary. They were supposed to be celibate. Different missionaries stayed at different times and went by foot preaching. They influenced all aspects of our lives at home to the extent that when I began to read love stories, these would be gently taken from my hands, the use of cosmetics was frowned upon and any sort of social life was regarded as ungodly. The congregation put them on a pedestal. When I was in my teens while doing my homework, a male missionary would come up to me and try to fondle my breasts. At other times when he found me running around in the house, he would catch me, pull me towards him and kiss me. I could feel his dick rise up in his sarong, trying to feel its way around. Feeling sick, I would push him away."

"Good God! fine sort of missionary," interposed Amber angrily. "Did you report him?"

"Of course not.I was not told the facts of life and what sex was all about. I just felt that his behaviour was not right, especially when he came up to me when he saw no one around. In any case no one would have believed me, for all who knew him had great respect for him. I am glad youngsters today are taught the facts of life at an early age."

Amber retorted, "fat lot of good it is doing them. Look at the rise of unmarried young mothers many of whom are having children out of choice, and are streetwise enough to know that the government will have to house and feed them. If the government clamped down on their benefits, there would be a decline of this. That money could go towards worthwhile causes like caring for the old, many of whom have contributed to the state in their early days."

Tim banged his fist on the table saying, "too damn right. The government needs to put its house in order. Look at the armed gangs mostly youths, parading London streets at night, using knives and guns, creating fear and causing death. I think twice about going out in the streets at night in case I get my throat slit. What sort of legal system do we have where the courts impose a ten year sentence, but is in effect for five years with the time in remand taken into consideration?"

Carol patted him on the shoulder and said, "where I come from, there is capital punishment, and while I don't condone with that, conditions at the prisons there are very different from those over here. Only basic meals are provided, the living conditions are just about bearable, and the inmates have to work. I have visited detention centres and prisons in Britain, in the course of my work, and whilst the buildings seem unwelcome, the inmates have opportunities for sports and gym, have access to television, counselling, worship and books to read Their food is reasonably good and varied. I can't swear to it but I have been told that many commit offences again on release, just to go back there. After all why not? There are no bills to pay and there is free food and lodging. Having said all this, there is a soft place in my heart for Britain, with its caring society, one of the first to respond generously with money for a worthy cause. Even little children would not think twice about digging into their piggy banks and giving the few coins they have saved."

A wave of panic swept over Amber's face suddenly, and she struck her fist on her forehead. "Folks you must love me and leave me. My parents will be arriving in an hour and I had earlier promised them a meal. I had completely forgotten about it. By all that's merciful, I hope I can rustle a meal in half an hour."

CHAPTER EIGHT

The commentary on the Television concerning Congo had come to an end, and it was about eleven in the night. Leon had indicated that he was ready for bed, but Carol said that she would switch off the Television when she was ready, and then go up to bed. He was finicky about how things were done in his house, and before he left, he showed her two remote controls and which buttons to press to turn off the television, as if she was some school child. Of course the plug had to be pulled out of the socket. Carol bit her tongue to prevent herself from screaming at him.

It was not as if the house was immaculate or tidy. Carol cast her eyes again over the living room. There was a green coloured sofa with two huge threatening armchairs, which seemed to take up a lot of space. Once one settled in one of the chairs, it was difficult to get up again, and Carol developed the habit of sitting on the edge of the chair in an upright position so that it made getting up easier. These were about twenty years old and looked ready for the scrap heap.

Talking of curtains, they stood there red and forbidding, shrouding the front and back windows and daring anyone to wash them. The huge carpet, a sort of beige when new, was punctuated with stains and weary with wear. Carol had once said to him in exasperation, "for God's sake, have some pride in your home and throw all these away. It is nice to have fresh curtains, a slightly modern sofa and some decent chairs. The carpet is crying for a painless death and to be relieved of its misery. If I am to spend some time here, I cannot live in these conditions."

Dear Leon was a man who did not like change, and now retired, liked nothing better than to potter about in the garden the whole day if possible, the weather permitting. Typical Englishman! The garden seemed a darn sight better than the inside of the house.

There was a lovely piano at one side of the room, and although able to play it well in early days, it was practically unused now as his work as a draughtsman left him incapacitated, and he could not use his fingers properly. On the piano top were photos on display of his three children and five grandchildren who, when scrutinised closely, appeared to smile maliciously. Except for his daughter who lived quite far away and could only pay yearly visits, those of the other children and their off springs were brief although they lived within easy distance. It was pathetic to see Leon's face light up with pleasure on the occasional times when they visited to boast of their achievements, or to present a photo of the family as if it was a golden trophy that had to be treasured and kept with pride of place.

There was no respect for their father or his friends. Charles, who had very long hair and untidy curls, would use a set of keys to come inside the house unannounced, although Carol had hinted that he should ring the bell first. Leon politely backed her but it was like pouring water over a duck's back. The only compromise he offered was to ring the bell, and then use the key to get in almost all at once!

Leon had been good to her and her children for twelve years since her husband's death. Marriage was on the cards but never seemed to materialise because they were incompatible and had different interests. Quite a lot of this had to do with their varied social and educational backgrounds prompting Carol often to laugh and say, "the only thing we have in common is that we like to go out and eat good food."

Carol sat on the sofa mesmerised by the

dwindling yellow flames of the fire in the living room. Having been just able to move on after her husband's death, she wanted to be free to do as she pleased, and to travel, which Leon hated. She switched off the television, turned off the gas fire and went upstairs. Which room was she going to, his room or the one next to his? She smiled to herself and decided to go to his room and lie next to him. What does it matter. He will be asleep anyway!

CHAPTER NINE

There are things that happen in this world of a terrestrial nature whose significance we may not understand, but that does not necessarily mean that they do not exist. The more educated one is, there is a tendency to pooh pooh the concept. For about a whole year after her husband's death, Carol had taken the children practically every day about twenty miles away to visit the grave. It was a fairly new graveyard, and the children would kneel beside the grave to tidy it and to clear any leaves that fell on it. Apart from putting flowers on the grave, she encouraged them to put a flower or two on nearby graves which seemed to be unattended. Very often as they used a small spade to tidy the sides of their father's grave, they would find a single one pound coin and would comment on this. Even the lovely soul Leon who befriended and then loved her and had taken her many times by car to the grave, would find the occasional coin. It was as if the dead was saying, "I will still look after you although I am gone." As for Carol she found nothing.

Her son and daughter saw sightings of her late husband either in the rooms at home, or occasionally when they visited a close friend at Hertfordshire.

One afternoon, before her daughter came home from school, Carol was lying on the bed when she felt a tight grip on the upper part of her right arm, and that area felt devoid of feeling. She thought to herself, "I must be getting a stroke." But the grip relaxed and when she tried to move her arm, she was able to do so.

It was not imagination, it was real. When her daughter came home, Carol hurried to her, related what had happened, and nervously stated that she did not know what to make of it. “Mum, it is the Holy Spirit,” she said simply.

Carol cast her mind back to her very early days, and recollected that on one occasion her father had told her that at every New Year’s Eve, he would get out his diary for the next year, and fill it up with all the things he intended to do throughout the year. One New Year’s Eve, he did the same thing. Her mother was preparing tea and he was sitting at the large kitchen table. Just then there was a loud sound like a stroke of a cane, and when he looked at the diary, there was a cane mark quite visible over the open page of the diary. Her mother was shocked at the sound. Her father never again attempted to fill up the diary in advance.

Carol used the living room as her bedroom. The windows were huge, and if she opened one, she could see who was at the door if she poked out her head. Occasionally she would hear the doorbell ring at intermittent times during the dead of night, and having been awakened from her sleep, she would call out, “who is it?” Opening one of the windows slightly so that she could be heard, she would repeat herself. There was no response. She would close the window, go back to bed and never thought much about it.

However when she was at her lowest ebb emotionally, she could hear the door bell ring during the day, only to find that there was no one there when she went to the door.

She remembered vividly the day when her daughter and young grandson came to stay. The door bell rang and the little one said, “I’ll get it,” and he rushed to the door to open it. He returned and said, “there’s no one there.”